DON'T FORGET TO REMEMBER

I wish, I wish
With all my heart
To fly with dragons
In a land apart.

D1254078

By Margaret Snyder
Illustrated by Don Williams
Based on the characters by Ron Rodecker

Visit Dragon Tales on the Web at www.dragontales.com

Watch us on PBS!

One lovely, lazy day in Dragon Land, Quetzal called Ord, Cassie, Zak, and Wheezie together. "Today we'll be working on a special school project," Quetzal said. "It is a *sorpresa*."

"I looooove surprises!" Wheezie shouted.

"*Bueno,*" Quetzal told her. "Good. But I will need your help."

Quetzal turned to Cassie. "Cassie, we will need something we can use to dig in the dirt. Can you find something like that?"

Cassie had her nose buried in a brand-new book. "Okay," she said as she turned the page.

"Ord," Quetzal said next, "I need you to fetch us a bucket of rainbow water."

"One bucket coming up," Ord said just as his stomach began to rumble. *A whole bucket of dragonberries sure would taste great right now,* he thought.

Last, Quetzal turned to Zak and Wheezie. "And you, *niños*—" he began.

"Whatever it is, *I* get to carry it," Wheezie interrupted.

"No, *I* will," Zak said.

"—please bring some giggle flowers for the class," Quetzal finished, shaking his head at the distracted dragons. "I'll see you all back here in a little while."

Zak and Wheezie were still arguing as Quetzal left.

"Okay, okay, you get to carry it," Zak finally said, "whatever it is! I can't remember anymore."

"Goggles, I think," said Wheezie, "made of glass."

Zak and Wheezie were still wondering about Quetzal's request when their friends Emmy and Max arrived.

"What are you two talking about?" Emmy asked.

Zak explained. "We think Quetzal asked for goggles made of glass," he ended.

"Maybe he meant swimming goggles," Max suggested. "I think Ord keeps a pair in his pouch."

Max went to find Ord, who was delighted to help. But that reminded Ord that he was supposed to get a bucket of *something* for Quetzal. He tried to remember what it was. Then it hit him.

"Max, can you help me pick a bucket of dragonberries?" Ord asked.

"Sure," said Max, and he and Ord raced off.

Meanwhile, Emmy asked Cassie what she had to get.

Cassie looked uneasy. "I don't know," she said. "I was reading my book, and I didn't really listen."

By then, Quetzal had returned. Zak and Wheezie raced toward him waving the swimming goggles. "We have the goggles made of glass," Wheezie sang.

"Goggles made of glass?" Quetzal replied. "But I asked for giggle flowers for the class."

When Ord and Max returned, they were carrying a bucket of dragonberries.

"Oh, Ord! I asked for a bucket of rainbow water," Quetzal said.

He turned to Cassie. "Cassie, did you find something we can use to dig?" he asked. Cassie sadly shook her head.

"Well, it looks like my *sorpresa* really *is* a surprise." Quetzal laughed ruefully. "We cannot do what I had planned with *these* things."

The dragons looked at their toes in embarrassment.

"Come now, *niños*," Quetzal said. "Let's try again. But this time I need everyone to listen carefully."

The dragons' faces brightened as they nodded.

"And with Max and Emmy's help, we can make the surprise even better," Quetzal added.

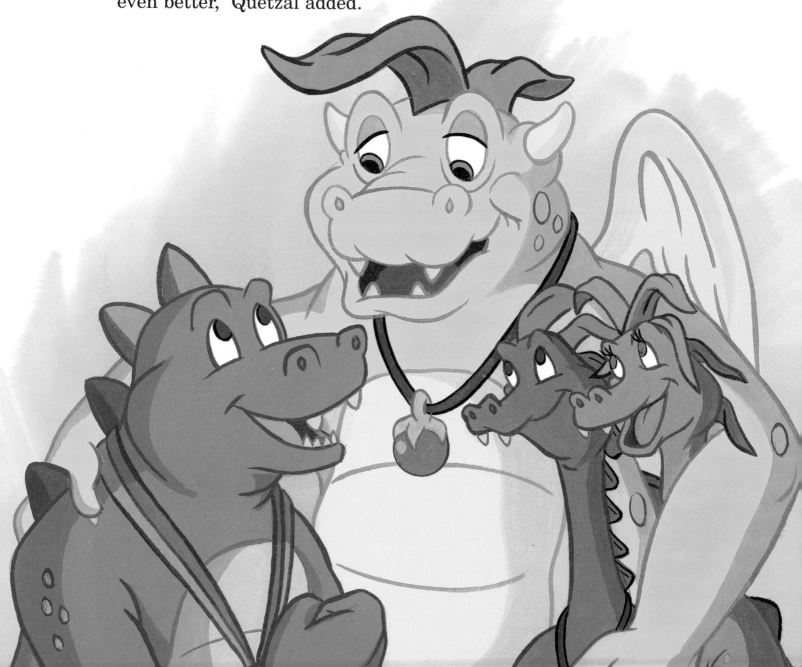

"So, one more time," Quetzal said. "Cassie, do you remember this time what to bring?"

"Something we can use to dig," Cassie said. She found a crayon and paper in her pouch, then drew a picture of a shovel. "This picture will help me remember," she added.

"Ord, you'll find us some rainbow water," Quetzal said.

Ord raced to the garden and returned with a watering can. "I'll use this," he said. "It's even better than a bucket and will remind me to get water instead of a snack."

"I hope we'll remember what *we're* supposed to bring," Zak told Wheezie in a worried voice. "Don't forget, it's giggle flowers."

"I've got an idea!" sang Wheezie. "I'll make up a rhyme to help us remember: Giggle flowers have wiggle powers." She giggled and wiggled happily.

"Emmy, we will also need some singing sunflowers," Quetzal instructed. "And from you, Max, some whispering willows. Remember to collect all the roots carefully so we can plant them again."

"We'll do it together," said Max. "That way, we can help each other remember what to get. Right, Emmy?"

"Definitely!" his sister agreed.

A short time later, everyone returned. Quetzal looked around happily at everything they carried.

"Excelente," he said with a big smile.

Then Quetzal described the surprise. "We are going to plant a garden. I asked Emmy and Max to help with more plants so now it can be an even more special *listening* garden," he explained.

"What's a listening garden?" Max asked.

"You will soon find out," Quetzal told him.

Everyone worked together to dig, plant, and water the garden. The magical flowers took root right away.

When the garden was finished, everybody stepped back to "ooh" and "aah" over it.

"Shush now and listen," Quetzal said softly. When everyone was quiet, they could hear the sunflowers singing, the willows whispering, and the giggle flowers gently laughing with each other.

"I think that every time you pass this garden, you will think about listening, *sí?*" Quetzal said.

Quetzal held up the bucket of berries and the goggles. "What should we do with these?" he asked, smiling.

Ord's stomach rumbled. "I don't know about the goggles," he replied, "but since we're all listening, let's listen to what my stomach is saying."

Quetzal laughed. "I forgot it was snack time."

"Not me," said Ord. "I never need help remembering *that*!"